This book belongs to

Dear Parents,

I've always dreamed about being a mother. Maybe because I was blessed with a great mother of my own. Thanks for everything, Mom!

Now that it's finally happened to me, it's even better than I ever could have imagined. And while I've had a great life filled with wonderful adventures, I've never felt more fulfilled, more myself, and—yes—more beautiful than I do now in my role as a mother.

This book is designed to celebrate the beauty of that special relationship with one's child and to encourage the wonder and awe we experience as we play and get to know each other.

ABOUT FACE is also intended to help you lay the groundwork for what I hope will be a lifetime of open communication. So don't hesitate to make silly faces or silly sounds as you read this book aloud. I promise, you and your child will both have fun!

Cindy Crawford

about face

Written by Ellen Schecter
Conceived by Cindy Crawford
Photographed by Jade Albert
Illustrated by Paul Harwood

HarperEntertainment
An Imprint of HarperCollins*Publishers*

Place a photograph of
you and your mommy
here

Face to face,
eye to eye,
heart to heart,
as the days go by.

You see me,
I see you—
that's how we learn
just what to do:
to love and to listen
day after day,
just you and me
in our own special way.

Heart to heart,
eye to eye,
face to face,
as the years go by.

Hello **NOSE**, hello toes; hello **LIPS** like a small, soft **ROSE**.

I **KISS** you and you kiss me, face to **FACE** like we like to be.

ABOUT FACE!

Now it's your turn.

Can you PUCKER up and kiss my nose?

Can you PUCKER up and

KISS my toes?

Come kiss my LIPS like

a RED, red rose.

Can you WIGGLE your toes while I wrinkle my NOSE?

Can you JIGGLE them, GIGGLE them,

HIGGLEDY-PIGGLE them?

YES, you can, you did it!

Hooray for your TOES, your sweet little toes,

all lined up in neat little ROWS!

How about that NOSE? That bright button nose!

Can you CRINKLE it, wrinkle it, hinkely-DINKLE it?

ABOUT FACE!

Now it's your turn to play.

What other TRICKS

can we do today?

Can you MIRROR ME, mirror me?
Watch what I do!

A SMILE'S just a frown
turned upside down—Can YOU do it, too?

Bet you can—YES, you can.
You can do it, it's true.

This is me CURIOUS,

this is me SAD.

This is me FURIOUS, this is me MAD.

This is me SILLY

this is me HAPPY.  This is me CHILLY,  this is me CLAPPY.

This is me GOOFY and googlely and glad

This is me woebegone, looking for DAD.

This is me
YUCKY
This is me
DUCKY

This is me
DRESSED UP

This is me
THINK-Y

This is me
MESSED UP

This is me
STINKY

Hey, this is **FUN.** Join in, everyone!

ABOUT FACE!

Now it's your TURN to
tell just how you feel —
It's easy, it's FUN—it's No Big Deal.

Just SPEAK with your eyes,
with a SMILE, or a POUT—
a whisper, a sputter, or even a SHOUT.

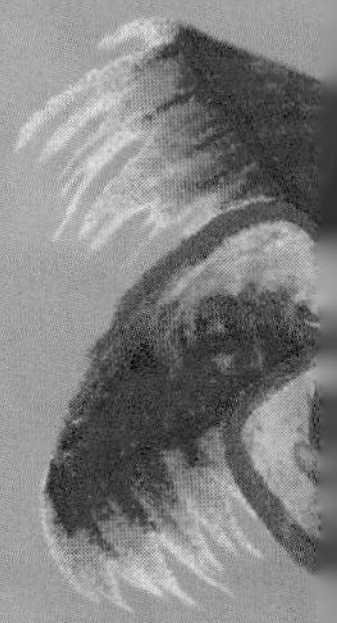

Are you feeling DIZZY? Or BUSY? Or all in a TIZZY?

Whatever feeling your FACE wants to show You can be sure MOMMY wants to know.

Those MOMMIES . . .

They follow you HERE,

they follow you THERE, they follow your

BABY FACE everywhere!

WHOOPS! Here she comes again.

Are you READY? Get set.

On the count of three

make your own FUNNY face

along with me!

Let's blow **BUBBLES** in doubles
just you and me.
We'll be **BUBBLY** buddies
floating high and free.

I'll look at you LOOKING at me,

two BUBBLY bub-buddies

TUB-BUBBLING with glee.

Can you be a monkey, a fish, or a BEAR
wearing fins or feathers instead of HAIR?
We can be anything we want to be.
We can pretend—
just follow me.

Scratch your head and armpits, TOO,
pretend we're living in the ZOO.

Peel a banana, swing from a TREE,
take a BITE, give one to me.
MONKEY see, monkey do. I'll go first—
Now you try, too.

I SCREAM, we scream,
MOMMY and me
want ICE CREAM!

A LICK for you, a LICK for me,
now we're SLIPPY-droppy-DRIPPY
as we can be.

I feed your FACE,
you feed mine,
SLURPY-sloppy ice cream
tastes S-O-O-O FINE.

Now let's play PEEKABOO, just YOU and me.

Let's PEEP through our fingers and pretend we can't see.

Let's BLOW dozens of KISSES

and catch every one.

Let's be GROWL-Y, prowl-y, howl-y, and jowl-y,

then share grrreat big bear HUGS when we're done.

ABOUT FACE,

Why don't you and your MOMMY join in the fun?

Too POOPED to pop?

Guess it's time to stop.

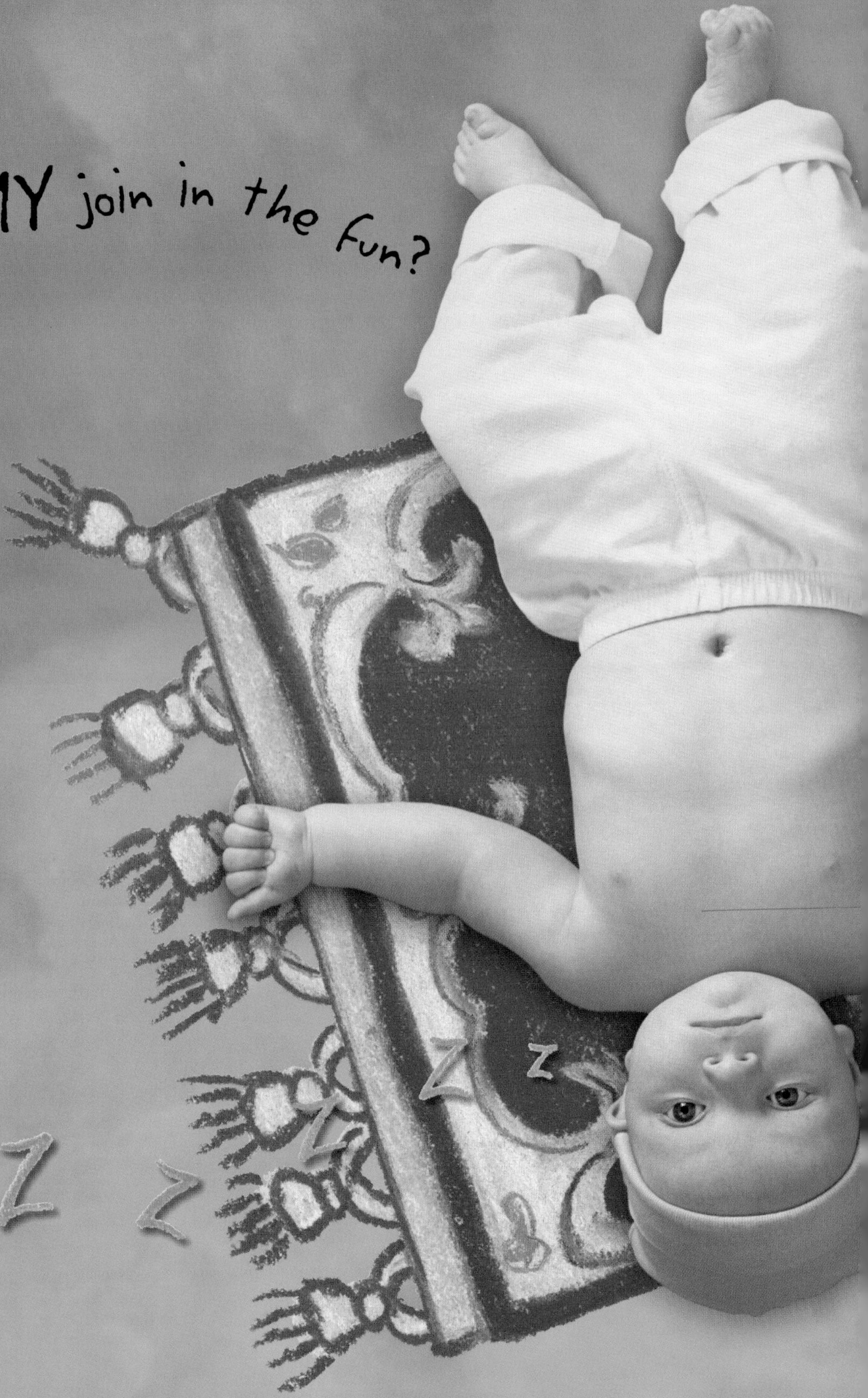

NAP time or night time,
CUDDLE-up-tight time,
turn-out-the-light time,
whisper-SLEEP-TIGHT time,
it's your time, it's my time,
it's SWEET DREAMS, good-night time.
SHHHHHHHHH!

FACE to FACE, eye to eye,
heart to HEART,
as the years go by.

DEAR PARENTS,

ABOUT FACE offers you dozens of delightful ways to play with your baby and to enjoy the ever-changing display of facial expressions, body language, and wordless sounds that lie at the heart of loving communication.

You may easily recognize tired whimpers, lazy yawns, or tiny fists rubbing closed eyes as signs of a sleepy baby who needs a back rub, a lullaby, or a quiet spot to sleep. But did you know that your child also expects you to reply to those many other coos, gurgles, and fleeting expressions sent your way? Even at the earliest ages, communication goes both ways. With this in mind, ABOUT FACE is designed to help you learn from your baby—to mirror, reflect, and, most important of all, to respond. It will engage you in real conversations even before your child masters the language spoken in your home.

Understanding and reacting to each other's nonverbal messages not only contributes to sensitive, creative play now, it can also help lay the foundation for your child's future emotional well-being. When you look, listen, and reply to your baby's many unspoken gestures, you are essentially telling your child, "I hear you. I'm here for you. You're safe. I love you."

In addition to establishing this bond of trust with your child, reading ABOUT FACE aloud will also teach and reinforce such essential social skills as taking turns, listening, leading, and following—laying the groundwork for later learning, especially reading and language skills.

Filled with wordplay and with varied rhythms and rhymes that will tickle your tongue as well as your child's ears, ABOUT FACE also encourages your child to fall in love with language. Reading, singing, and talking to children not only delights them, it builds strong vocabularies, helping babies understand the meanings of many words even before they can say them.

Because children of different ages will enjoy different parts of ABOUT FACE in different ways, we suggest you experiment as you go. You could: [A] read the whole book [B] just read the parts you like best [C] talk about the pictures without reading the words, or [D] ask your child to "read" the book to you. "Pretend reading" is a very important step toward real reading, so encourage it!

Remember, there is no single way to delight in this book. Some children will like to chime in with favorite words or phrases. Others will prefer to play the same games every time. You and your child may even invent your own games based on the ones you find here. Simply follow your child's lead and have as much fun playing with each other as Cindy Crawford and her son, Presley, so clearly do.

All of us involved in creating this book genuinely hope you enjoy ABOUT FACE and this wonderful period of growth for both you and your child. We especially hope you will savor these special moments with your child—face to face, eye to eye, and heart to heart—today and as the many years go by.

Ellen Schecter

ABOUT FACE.

Printed in China.

For information address HarperCollins Publishers Inc., 10 East 53rd Street, New York, NY 10022.

HarperCollins books may be purchased for educational, business, or sales promotional use. For information please write: Special Markets Department, HarperCollins Publishers Inc., 10 East 53rd Street, New York, NY 10022.

FIRST EDITION

Conceived by Cindy Crawford
Written by Ellen Schecter
Photographed by Jade Albert
Illustrated by Paul Harwood
Art Directed and Designed by Jo Obarowski
Produced by Hope Innelli
Associate Produced by Katherine O'Leary
Makeup for Ms. Crawford by Sonia Kashuk
Hairstyling for Ms. Crawford by Kevin Mancuso
Wardrobe styling by Kristen Valentino
Children's grooming by Rita Saranchak for Parella Management
Children's clothing provided in part by Babystyle.com

Printed on acid-free paper

Library of Congress Cataloging-in-Publication Data has been applied for.

ISBN 0-06-017830-2

01 02 03 04 05 SCP 10 9 8 7 6 5 4 3 2 1

Special
thanks to our baby models:
Brandon Heller, Mariah Johnson (A+
Models), Victoria Parnell, Gabriella Granata
(Abrams Artists Agency), Dylan Burke (Big Shots Model
Management), Tatyanna Fry, Jordan Barry (Cunningham
Escott Dipene), Alexa Walter, Anthony Arca, Karim Sullivan
(Elaine Gordon Model Management), Gabrielle Quinones
(Ford Models, Inc.), Kacar (Funny Face Today), Peter Oh (Mollo
Management), Hunter McClain, Malcom McClain, Max Singer (Schuller
Talent), Gerhard Rahn, Addis DeFazio, Cody Werner, Finn Manning
(Product Model Management), and, of course, Presley Gerber.
Additional thanks to our crew and support team: Peggy Albert,
Alexander Altman, Anna Altman, Jim Altman, Allison Candage,
Luiza Desouza, Victoria Escalle, Jim Levine, Mary McAdam
Keane, Christopher McCormack, Denise Mitchell, Tim
Rhoades, Meryl Salzinger, Renato Seixas, Adam
Sobel, Laumont Labs, and to our child
development and parenting consultant,
Leni Winn, CSW.